I, MOUSE

by

ROBERT KRAUS

WINDMILL BOOKS & DUTTON
NEW YORK

for BRUCE

Copyright 1978 by Robert Kraus · All rights reserved · No part of
this book may be reproduced or transmitted in any form or by any means,
electronic or mechanical, including photocopying, recording or by any in-
formation storage and retrieval system, without permission in writing from
the Publisher. Windmill Books and Dutton, 2 Park Avenue, New York,
New York 10016 · Library of Congress catalog card number 77-25293
· Library of Congress Cataloging in Publication Data ·
Kraus, Robert · I, Mouse · A mouse relates how he goes from house
nuisance to house hero · (1. Mice—Fiction) I. Title · PZ7.K868Iac
· 1978 · (E) 77-25293 · ISBN 0-525-62328-0 · Published
simultaneously in Canada by Clark, Irwin and Company, Limited,
Toronto and Vancouver · Printed in U.S.A. · First Edition ·
10 9 8 7 6 5 4 3 2 1

I am a mouse.

Cats chase me.

People set traps to catch me.

Is it my fault I'm a mouse?

I like to munch on cheese. Is that a crime?

I like to dance with other mice.

I like people.

But people don't like me.

I live in a big house

with a mother, father, and a little boy.

But they're always setting traps to catch me.

I'm clever, though, and they haven't caught me yet.

Knock on wood.

If I could only think of a way to make them like me.

One morning, their alarm clock didn't go off, so I
woke them up, but it was Sunday.

I tried to join in their songs, but they thought I was
just squeaking.

I even tried to help wash the dishes, but the mother
shooed me away.

I can dance just as well as that mouse on television, but the little boy prefers to watch him.

Good grief! A burglar just came through the
window.

Immediately I throw myself at him and bite his
ankle as hard as I can.

We fall to the floor and I stand on his chin and punch his nose.

The coward pulls a knife,

so I bite his wrist as hard as I can.

The noise of the scuffle awakens the family and they hurry downstairs.

"Please call off your mouse," cries the burglar.
"He's a terror."

"Good mouse," says the mother.
"Brave mouse," says the father.
"Watchmouse!" says the little boy.

The little boy shakes my hand.
I am so proud and happy.

The burglar says he is sorry. But as he broke the
law he is sent to jail anyway.

They put my picture in all the papers and I receive thirty-eight fan letters, all of which I answer personally.

Best of all the family loves me now, and that, with a little cheese, is really all a mouse's heart desires.